W9-BJV-003
Juvenile Historical
Collection
A Gift Of
Martha Bennett King
The Denver Public Library
DENVER PUBLIC LIBRARY
R02008 07373

The Steel Flea

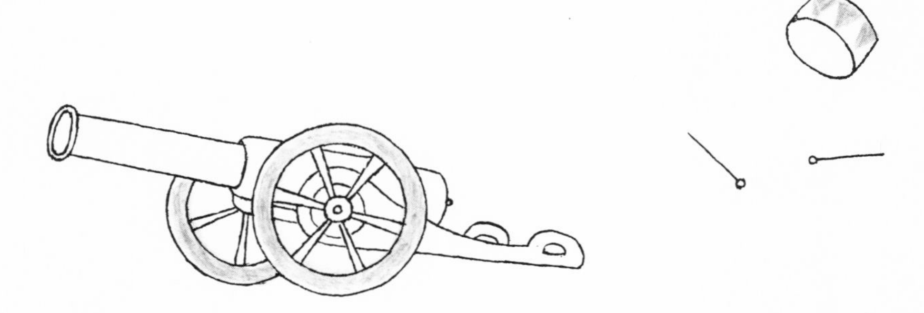

HARPER & ROW, PUBLISHERS NEW YORK, EVANSTON, AND LONDON

The Steel Flea

A STORY BY
NICHOLAS LESKOV

ADAPTED FROM THE RUSSIAN BY
BABETTE DEUTSCH AND
AVRAHM YARMOLINSKY

REVISED EDITION

PICTURES BY JANINA DOMANSKA

R02008 07373

THE STEEL FLEA

Text copyright © 1943, 1964 by Babette Deutsch and Avrahm Yarmolinsky
Pictures copyright © 1964 by Janina Domanska

Printed in the United States of America. All rights reserved. No part of this book may be used or reproduced in any manner whatsoever without written permission except in the case of brief quotations embodied in critical articles and reviews. For information address Harper & Row, Publishers, Incorporated, 49 East 33rd Street, New York 16, N.Y.

REVISED EDITION

Library of Congress catalog card number: 64-11837

jFIC
LESKOV
N

The Steel Flea

THE war was over. The Russians had chased the invaders, shaking and shivering, out of the country. They had proven a match for the terrible Napoleon himself. Alexander, Emperor of all the Russias, had come to Vienna to sign the peace treaty. He signed it, without even one little blot, and was feeling very spry.

"Platov," he said to the Cossack chief who attended him, "let us not go home at once. It is our wish to travel farther and behold the marvels of the Western World."

Now General Platov, like many another good Cossack, was born and bred beside the waters of the quiet Don. All the bones of his body, not to mention his heart, his liver, and his lights, were crying to go back there. He wanted to sit once more on the banks of the quiet Don, to eat buckwheat grits cooked with plenty of lard, a fat sturgeon, and boiled sucking pig with horseradish and sour cream. He wanted to eat the good black bread and drink the heady wine of the Don and go to sleep in his own bed in his own house on his own broad acres. In short, Platov was homesick.

"Sire," he said to the Czar, "we have been away from Russia a long time now. The country needs your Majesty." Platov did not mention the buckwheat grits or the boiled sucking pig or the black bread. He thought such homely fare might not please the imperial palate. But he tried hard to persuade the Czar to go home.

The Czar, however, paid no attention. He was full of curiosity. He set out forthwith, and Platov, willy-nilly, had to go along. Wherever they went, Platov looked on grumpily.

It was always the same. The Czar would no sooner arrive in a new country than he had to go to visit all the museums and arsenals and mills. He was most affable. He was delighted with every new piece of work that was shown him. He exclaimed over the clever workmanship. He praised the delicate machinery. He admired every cog and wheel and gear. The members of his retinue would stand by in silence. Only Platov would snort with disgust.

"Sire," he would grumble, "we have better things at

home." But Platov's snorts made no difference to his imperial master. The Czar continued to praise the foreigners. He really liked their inventions. And besides, it was good politics to be friendly to these foreign nations. But Platov did not care about that.

Now the story of Emperor Alexander, and of his interest in things foreign, traveled on before him. In good time it reached England. So that when the Czar arrived, the English were prepared to show him the most remarkable tools and weapons and inventions of all kinds that they could produce. They were glad of the chance to prove that they could outdo the Russians.

As usual, the Czar was full of admiration for everything that they brought out. As usual, Platov looked on and sulked.

"Sire," he said with a snort, "we have better things at home."

One day when Platov went to bid the Czar good morning, his Majesty greeted him with these words: "Today we are going to visit a sugar refinery."

"Sire," Platov objected, "haven't we visited factories enough? Haven't we seen foreign things aplenty? Isn't it, begging your Majesty's pardon, but isn't it time to go home?"

"No," said the Czar. His tone was gracious but it was also firm. "No. It is our pleasure to see all that is to be seen in foreign parts. And do you know, Platov, I have heard that they make really excellent sugar here."

There was nothing else to do. Platov had to accompany his Majesty to the sugar refinery. The English showed the Czar various kinds of sugar: brown and white sugar, granulated sugar and powdered sugar, little sparkling lumps of sugar, and a sugar loaf as tall as a steeple. They invited him to taste it. And so he did. Had it been polite, he would have smacked the imperial lips, but he merely murmured: "Delicious!"

All of a sudden Platov burst out: "And where is the Bobrinsky sugar?" The English were taken aback. They began to nudge each other and whisper to each other: "Bobrinsky . . . Bobrinsky . . ."

And finally they had to admit that though they had all kinds of sugar, they had no Bobrinsky.

Platov bridled and snorted.

"Well, then," he said, "what are you bragging about? You come to Russia and we'll give you tea with real Bobrinsky sugar, and then you'll know what sugar is, I can tell you!"

The Czar pulled Platov by the sleeve.

"Please," he said quietly. "Don't spoil my politics!"

So Platov said no more.

That night the Emperor said to Platov: "Tomorrow we're going to visit an arsenal. The English have weapons of war there that put our Russian workmanship to shame."

Platov did not answer. He could not. He stuck his

humped nose into his shaggy cloak, went to his lodgings, commanded his orderly to fetch him a bottle of Caucasian vodka, tossed it off, said his prayers before the holy image that traveled with him, covered himself with his cloak, and snored so that no Englishman in the house could sleep.

Early the next morning the Czar and Platov set out for the arsenal.

They drove for some distance and at last they came to a huge building. The entrance hall was immense. The corridors were so long that the other end was lost in haze.

The Englishmen at once began to show the Czar various instruments and weapons of war, and they explained the uses of each. The Czar glanced at Platov to see if he was impressed. But Platov walked on with his eyes lowered, seeing nothing. He only twirled the ends of his mustachios until they formed rings.

At last the Czar said to him: "My dear Platov, what is the matter? Why are you silent? Aren't you astonished by all this? Don't you marvel at these English?"

"Sire," replied Platov, "the only thing I marvel at is that our Don Cossacks fought without all this and beat the boots off the armies of twelve nations."

"Nonsense," said the Emperor.

"I dare not argue with your Majesty," said Platov sulkily, "but that is a fact, and there's no getting around it."

The Englishmen, seeing that the Emperor was scolding his attendant, felt that they must intervene. They led the

Emperor before a gigantic statue of Mars, and taking a carbine from one of the statue's hands and a pistol out of the other, they begged his Majesty to examine them. The Czar looked at the carbine, but he remained calm, because he had one like it at home. Then they drew his attention to the pistol.

"This pistol, your Majesty," said the Englishmen, "is extraordinary. Nowhere else will you find such workmanship. One of our admirals pulled it out of the belt of a pirate chief in Candelabria."

The Emperor looked at the pistol. Indeed, it was extraordinary.

"Ah!" he exclaimed, "how beautifully this is made!" Then, turning to Platov, he said, "If I had such a master gunsmith in Russia, it would make me truly proud and happy. I would ennoble him at once."

Platov put his hand into the pocket of his wide trousers and pulled out a gunsmith's screwdriver.

"This pistol doesn't unscrew," said the Englishmen.

But without paying any attention to them, Platov began to pick the lock of the pistol. He turned it once. He turned it twice. The lock opened and Platov invited the Czar to look at the trigger. On the inner curve there was an inscription in Russian: "Made by Ivan Moskvin in the city of Toola, Russia."

The Englishmen's faces got very red. The extraordinary

pistol that their admiral had captured from the pirate chief was of Russian make. They began to whisper among themselves: "That's one on us!"

At this the Czar turned to Platov and said sadly: "Why did you have to embarrass these Englishmen? Come, let us be off."

So they said good-bye and drove away.

That evening the Czar went to a ball. He loved dancing even more than he loved foreign inventions. As for Platov, he told his orderly to open another bottle of Caucasian vodka, and he tossed it off and said his prayers and went to bed. But he could not sleep. He was glad to think that he had got the better of the English and that he had put the gunsmiths of the city of Toola in the right light. But at the same time he felt badly.

"Why," he said to himself, "did the Czar have to be sorry for the Englishmen? I don't understand it."

And in this mood he got up twice, crossed himself, drank a good dose of Caucasian medicine, and so managed to fall into a deep slumber.

That night the Englishmen did not sleep well either. They were disturbed over what had happened at the arsenal. They felt that they had to make up for it somehow. So while the Czar was enjoying himself at the ball the Englishmen contrived a new marvel which would surprise him and which would at the same time take the wind out of Platov's sails.

THE next day the Englishmen invited the Emperor to visit a steel mill. They took him through one room after another and showed him machines and tools and all sorts of steel articles. The Czar nodded and smiled, but said nothing.

"Thank heaven!" Platov said to himself. "Everything is all right. His Majesty has not marveled at anything here. Maybe at last he'll be willing to go home?"

But then they walked into the last room. And there the English workmen were standing in their aprons and holding a silver tray on which there was nothing at all. The Czar looked puzzled. They were presenting him with an empty tray!

"Pray, accept it," murmured the English workmen. "This is our humble gift to your Majesty."

"But what is it?" asked the Czar, bewildered.

"May it please your Majesty to look at this speck."

The Emperor stared harder, and indeed there on the tray he saw the tiniest possible speck, which sparkled in the light.

"May it please your Majesty," said the English workmen, "to spit on the royal finger and take up the speck and place it on the royal palm."

"But," said the Czar in amazement, "what do I want this speck for?"

"Ah, but you see, your Majesty," they said then, "it is not a speck. It is a nymphusoria, commonly known as a flea."

"Is it alive?" asked the Czar. Because, to tell the truth, his Majesty, while graciously interested in English inventions and museum pieces and even stuffed animals, had no desire to be bitten by a flea.

"No, your Majesty," the English workmen hastened to inform him. "She is not alive. She was forged by us out of pure English steel. And in her middle there is a spring by means of which you wind her up. May it please your Majesty to turn the key and she will begin to dance a quadrille."

The Czar's curiosity was aroused.

"But where is the key?" he asked eagerly.

"Right before your Majesty's eyes."

"Then why don't I see it?" asked the Czar.

"Because," said the English workmen, "in order to see it, a microscope is required."

Whereupon they brought out a microscope and offered it to the Emperor, and he bent over it and saw that, indeed, on the tray beside the tiny flea there was an even tinier key.

"May it please your Majesty," said the English workmen, "to take up the flea. In her middle there is a spring. Insert the key, wind it seven times, and the flea will begin to dance."

With some difficulty the Czar managed to get hold of the key and to grasp it with the august fingers of his right hand. He held the tiny flea in the fingers of the left hand, and no sooner did he insert the key in her middle than he felt her stir her whiskers. Then she began to twiddle her feet. And finally, when he had turned the key seven times, she leaped into the air and began to dance. She took two steps to the right and two steps to the left, and thus she danced an entire quadrille in five figures.

The Czar was so enchanted that he at once commanded that the English workmen be given a million in any kind of currency they liked: silver five-kopek pieces or small bills. The English asked to be given silver.

Platov was very much annoyed with them, but he said nothing. He only grumbled to himself: "It is very strange. They present his Majesty with this steel flea, and they get a million in silver for it. And they don't even give his Majesty a case in which to keep the flea. Every article comes in a case. Ugh, these English!"

The English overheard Platov's words.

"There is a case for the flea," they said. "Yes, indeed. It is a hollow walnut carved out of a whole diamond."

"Very suitable," Platov admitted.

"But you see we cannot part with it," said the Englishmen, "because the diamond is one of the Crown jewels. We are very sorry, but what belongs to the English Crown cannot be sold, even to the Emperor of all the Russias."

Platov got very angry.

"Crown jewel or no Crown jewel, you cannot keep an article without a case. A tiny thing like this will be lost before you can say 'knife.' An article always comes in a case!" growled Platov. "They are cheats, that's what they are!"

"Never mind," said the Emperor. "Don't spoil my politics! That is the English way of doing things." Then he turned to the Englishmen and asked with his usual graciousness: "And pray, what is that diamond walnut worth in which the flea is kept?"

The Englishmen said it was worth five thousand.

"Of course," said his Majesty, "you cannot sell one of the Crown jewels. But perhaps it could be given away—for a consideration—say, five thousand?"

The Englishmen agreed.

So Platov, frowning but helpless, gave them another five thousand, and they presented the Czar with the diamond walnut. The Czar placed the flea inside of it, and the key too, and then for safekeeping he put the diamond walnut in his golden snuffbox and ordered that the golden snuffbox be placed in his traveling case, which was lined with ivory and mother-of-pearl and was wrapped in green velvet.

Then the Emperor dismissed the English workmen with honor, saying graciously: "You are master craftsmen, the best in the whole world, and my Russians can do nothing to compare with your work."

The English were very much pleased. As for Platov, in the presence of the Czar he could say nothing. But without a word he took the microscope and put it in his trouser pocket. "Because," he said to himself, "it belongs with the article, and these Englishmen have got enough money from us already."

The only satisfaction he had was that at last the Czar consented to go home.

On the way there, however, the Czar and Platov had very little agreeable conversation, because they were of different minds.

"These English," said the Czar admiringly, "are certainly masters. Nobody can hold a candle to them."

"But," argued Platov, "our workmen, your Majesty, only need to look at a thing in order to make it, and improve on it, too."

When they had traveled a little farther, the Czar, shaking his head in wonder, said again: "These English are the finest craftsmen in the world."

"The only trouble with our Russian workers, your Majesty," said Platov, suppressing a snort, "is that they have not been properly taught. But really—"

"No, Platov," said his Majesty, "say what you like, the English are tops."

Platov could not openly disagree with the Emperor, but he was so mortified that whenever their coach drew up at a station, he got out, tossed off a tumbler of vodka, ate a pretzel, lit his pipe, which held a full pound of tobacco, and began to smoke. Then he would go back to the coach and sit down beside the Czar, as mum as an oyster. The Czar would look out of one window, and Platov would stick his pipe out of the other window and blow smoke into the wind. In this fashion they at last reached the capital.

As soon as they got there, the Czar dismissed Platov, saying: "You smoke so much that my brain is sooty."

Platov was offended. He went home, ate a whole sucking pig with horseradish and sour cream and drank a couple of bottles of Don wine, but all this did not help. He went on brooding over the triumph of the English. And in this glum mood he lay down on a couch and smoked his pipe.

THE marvelous flea made of English steel remained in the Emperor's traveling case until the day of his death. Just before his end he gave it to the priest who was performing the last rites, bidding him show it to the Empress when her first sorrow was over.

In due time the priest gave it to the Empress. She watched the flea dance the quadrille, and she even smiled at its antics, but then she shook her head, saying: "I am a widow now, and entertainments are not for me. Let this curio be given to my dear husband's successor, his brother Nicholas, with the rest of the imperial jewels."

The Emperor Nicholas had a good deal of trouble on his hands when he ascended the throne, and so at first he paid no attention to the little steel flea. But one day he happened to look over the traveling case that his brother had left him, and he opened the snuffbox and found the diamond nut, and inside that lay the steel flea. She had not been wound up for a long time, and so she lay there, meek and motionless. Emperor Nicholas, seeing merely a speck, looked at it in astonishment.

"What have we here?" he asked. "Why did our brother take such care of this?"

"Your Majesty," said the courtiers, "we have no idea what it is. It is not worth keeping, your Majesty."

"No," said Emperor Nicholas, "our brother evidently valued it. We must find out about it."

"Your Majesty," said one of the older courtiers, "there is a pharmacist who has a shop opposite the Anichkov Bridge. He is accustomed to weighing poisons on very fine scales. He is used to handling delicate things. Perhaps your Majesty would care to have him called in."

"By all means," said Emperor Nicholas.

So they summoned the pharmacist and showed him the steel flea.

He took it between finger and thumb and put it on the tip of his tongue.

"It feels cold," he said, "as though it were made of some powerful metal."

Then he tested it daintily with his teeth.

"Believe it or not," he said, taking it out of his mouth and

squinting at it, "it is a flea. It is not a real flea. It is made of metal. And it is not Russian work, either."

Emperor Nicholas at once commanded that they find out where the steel flea came from and what it was for.

So the records were duly examined, but nowhere was there a line about the steel flea. Then they started making inquiries, but nobody knew anything about it.

Fortunately, Platov was still alive. In fact, the Don Cossack was still lying on his couch and smoking his pipe. And at last, word came to his ears about the excitement in the palace over the steel flea. So Platov rose from his couch, threw away his pipe, put on all his medals, and went to the capital to appear before Emperor Nicholas.

"Brave old man," said Emperor Nicholas, "what do you wish?"

"Your Majesty," replied Platov, "I wish nothing for myself. I have my broad acres on the quiet Don. I have all the food and drink I desire. I have sufficient tobacco as well. I am perfectly satisfied."

"Why, then, are you here?" asked the Czar.

"I have come," answered Platov, "simply to tell you about this steel flea that has been found. I know the whole story. Indeed, it happened before my very eyes."

So he told Emperor Nicholas all about it, and finally he said: "And if it please your Majesty, there is also a key with which to wind up the flea. But in order to see the key, it is necessary to use a microscope. However, I have their microscope right here in my pocket."

With these words, he pulled out the microscope, and they saw the key and stuck it into the hole in the flea's middle and wound her up. No sooner was she wound up, than she leaped into the air and began to dance: two steps to the right, two steps to the left, and so on through a whole quadrille in five figures.

"Remarkable!" exclaimed Emperor Nicholas. "Truly remarkable!"

Platov snorted, so loudly that the ladies of the court jumped.

"Your Majesty," he said then, "it is remarkable. But let's not make too much of it. Our Russian workmen have nothing to be ashamed of."

"Have our Russian workmen made something like this?" asked the Emperor.

"Not exactly," Platov admitted. "But we ought to show this steel flea to our gunsmiths in Toola or some such place. I'll wager they have only to look at it and they will do a better job. The English won't be so uppity then. Our Russian masters can outdo the English any day in the week and twice on Thursdays."

Emperor Nicholas stroked his mustache thoughtfully. He was struck by Platov's idea. He did not like to think that his Russian folk were in any way inferior to foreigners.

So he said to Platov: "Those are wise words. You shall be put in charge of this matter. We are occupied with affairs of State and we do not need this little curio just now. Take it with you, and the key too, in its diamond walnut case in the imperial snuffbox. Go back to your quiet Don and enjoy life as a brave old soldier should."

"Thank you, Sire," said Platov.

"And on your way," the Czar went on, "stop off at Toola and show the gunsmiths of Toola this little article. Let them examine it and see what they can do to improve it. Tell them the whole story: that our late brother admired it and praised the foreigners who made it; but tell them, too, that their present Czar puts his trust in his own people, for the Russians are no worse than anybody else. They will heed our word, and will make us proud of them, we know."

PLATOV was pleased. He took the steel flea and set out for the quiet Don, and on his way there he stopped off to show the Toola gunsmiths the flea and give them Emperor Nicholas's message.

"Well," he said, when he had finished, "what about it, my good men? What about the gracious word of our Emperor Nicholas?"

"Little Father," they answered, "we are grateful."

"And what will you do," demanded Platov, "to deserve the trust that his Majesty puts in you?"

"We can't tell you right now," said the Toola gunsmiths. "The English aren't fools," they added. "In fact, they're a clever lot. If you want to outdo them, you must take thought."

"Blockheads!" roared Platov. "You must take thought, eh? If our Czar wants any thinking done, he has the whole Academy of Sciences to do it for him. You are gunsmiths. Get down to brass tacks. Tell me what you are going to make."

The Toola workmen were insulted.

"If your Honor doesn't care to leave the English flea with us," they said, "very well. There are enough fleas in Toola without her."

"I'll take her to the gunsmiths at Izhevsk," said Platov angrily. "They'll show our Czar what his people can do."

At these words the pride of the Toola workmen was touched.

"Take it, then," they said. "But your Honor will have a long way to go to get to Izhevsk."

"I ride fast," answered Platov shortly.

"Yes," said the Toola workmen then, "these gunsmiths at Izhevsk may be smart fellows. But they've nobody like Lefty here. There's a gunsmith for you! Why, he can take you apart and oil you and screw you together again as good as new. Maybe better."

"Oh," said Platov. "So? You believe that Lefty could . . ."

"Only trust us," said the Toola workmen. "Go your way

to your home on the quiet Don and leave this steel flea here with us, just as it is, in the diamond walnut in the golden snuffbox."

"And what then?" asked Platov.

"Take your ease on the banks of the quiet Don. Heal the wounds your Honor has received for our fatherland."

"And what then?" Platov repeated impatiently.

"When you are ready to go back to the capital, stop off here and send for us. By that time, with God's help, we'll have something to show you."

Platov snorted.

"Well," he conceded at last, "have it your own way. I trust you. Only make sure you don't go and substitute some piece of gimcrack jewelry for this diamond walnut. And whatever you do, be careful not to spoil the fine English work on the steel flea."

Then Platov turned up the collar of his cloak and twirled his mustachios and was about to leave the place. But before going he turned round once more and said: "Don't be too long about it, either. I ride fast. Before a month is up I'll be leaving my quiet Don and traveling back to St. Petersburg. And I must have something capital to show the Czar when I get there."

"Set your mind at rest, Little Father," they said. "We won't spoil the English workmanship. And we'll give you back the very same diamond walnut. A month is more than enough time. And when you get back here, we'll have something for you to show the Emperor. Exactly what we can't just say."

Platov had to be content with that. He couldn't know that they had thought up something so extraordinary that if they had even hinted at it, he wouldn't have believed them.

Platov had no sooner left Toola than three of the most skillful workmen took the matter in hand. One of them was a left-handed fellow who was squint-eyed and had a mole on his left cheek. And this Lefty had no hair on his temples, because it had all been pulled out in the days when he was an apprentice. But he was so clever that he could take you apart and oil you and screw you together again as good as new. Maybe better.

The three did not set to work at once. Each of them put some bread, some salt, and a couple of onions into a bundle. And Lefty's old mother saw to it that he had a little pie, too. Then the three took leave of their comrades and of their loving families. And then without another word they disappeared from Toola.

"They have run out on us!" cried a gloomy old gunsmith. "They were bragging for nothing. And they've taken the royal snuffbox besides, and the diamond walnut and the steel flea!"

The people of Toola were dismayed. But Lefty's old mother scolded them roundly for doubting her son.

"Only wait!" she wound up. "They'll come back. And they'll do themselves proud. You'll see, you thickheads!"

As a matter of fact, the three gunsmiths had gone on a pilgrimage. They were bound for the town of Mtzensk to pray before the image of St. Nicholas there. In times beyond the memory of living men this stone image had miraculously floated down the river, borne on a large stone cross. It was a full-length image of the saint, his face dark, his robes parcel-gilt. In one hand he held a model of a church, perfect in every detail. In the other hand he held a sword, signifying victory. The saint was the patron of gunsmiths. The three from Toola had a mass served before the image of St. Nicholas and another mass before the stone cross that had carried him down the river. Then, in the dead of night, they returned home.

At once they went to Lefty's house.

"Mother," said Lefty, "we have work to do. I must ask you to take yourself off. Go next door and stay with my godmother."

Lefty's mother looked at him and was satisfied that he had business in which she could be of no help. But before she left she said: "You must be hungry. Let me fetch you something to eat."

"No, Mother," Lefty answered. "We have no time to eat now. Good-bye." And he put his hands on her shoulders and pushed her respectfully out of the house. Then he bolted the door, latched the shutters, mended the light before a small image of St. Nicholas that hung in the corner, and with his two companions set to work.

A WHOLE day went by without a sign from Lefty and his comrades. The door remained bolted, the shutters remained latched. The folk of Toola crowded about the house, wondering what the three clever gunsmiths were about. They saw nothing but the smoke that rose out of the chimney. They heard only the sound of tiny hammers ringing on the anvils. The sound teased the ears of the folk of Toola.

"What are they up to in there?" they asked Lefty's mother.

But she only shook her head sagely and answered: "Wait and see." She did not want them to think that she knew no more than anybody else.

"There must be some way of finding out what is happening in there," said the folk of Toola.

So they hit upon a plan. They sent a boy with a small brazier and told him to knock on the door and ask to borrow some live coals to start the oven going.

"With all that hammering and forging, they must have plenty of live coals and to spare," they said.

The boy took the brazier and knocked at the door. But there was no answer. He banged on the shutters. But still there was no answer. So at last the boy went away.

The hammering went on inside the house all that day and even during the night.

"But what do they live on?" asked the folk of Toola. "Working as hard as they do, they need food."

And so the Toola folk hit upon another plan for satisfying their curiosity. They sent one of the women with a bowl of cabbage soup and a platter of little pies to Lefty's mother.

"Take this to your son," she said. "You had no time to cook anything for him before you left the house."

So Lefty's mother took the soup and the little pies and knocked on the shutters.

"Here," she said, "is something tasty. Open the shutters and take it before it cools."

Lefty would have paid no attention, but his comrades were hungry and they begged him to listen to his mother and accept the gift of food.

"Open the shutter a crack, Lefty," they said, "and let her shove it in."

But Lefty shook his head.

"My mother is a fine woman," he said, "but even my mother is a woman, and full of curiosity. As for the others, they can't wait to see what we are doing. I can hear them out there crowding about the window. I can almost hear them craning their necks. If we open the shutters even a crack, they will peek in. Then our secret will be known all over town."

"But Lefty," pleaded the other two, "we can work faster if we have something to eat."

"Very well," said Lefty, "let them rig up a pulley and lower the soup and the little pies down to us through the chimney."

And so it was done. And though the food had cooled a bit while they were arguing and rigging up the pulley, it got quite warm again on its journey down the warm chimney. And if it got a little sooty too, why that only made it taste more like real Toola food. Nor did they stop work while they ate, but ladled in the soup and the pies with one hand and hammered with the other.

So another day went by, and another night. And still the folk of Toola were consumed with curiosity.

Finally one of the neighbors thought up a scheme.

They went and stood in front of Lefty's house and shouted: "Fire! Fire! Fire!"

They were sure the three would get scared and open the door, and their secret would be out.

And indeed Lefty did open the shutters and stick out his head. But it completely blocked the opening.

"Your godmother's house is burning!" cried the neighbors.

"Let it burn!" he replied. "We can't be bothered."

And he pulled his head in again, slammed the shutter, latched it securely, and went on with his work.

The good folk of Toola got no satisfaction. Lefty and his comrades let no one have a glimpse of them and said not another word. And this went on until Platov returned.

GENERAL Platov had taken his ease on the banks of the quiet Don. But once he climbed into his coach for the return journey, he was impatient to get to Toola. He sat in the coach, and the coachman sat on the box, and on either side of the coachman sat a Cossack with a nagaika, which is a Cossack whip. The Cossacks whipped the coachman, and the coachman whipped the horses. And when, as sometimes happened, one of the Cossacks dozed off, Platov himself gave him a kick from behind and the Cossack leaped up and whipped the coachman harder than before, and the coachman laid it into the horses and they tore along faster than ever. In fact, this arrangement was so successful that the horses could never halt when they came to a station, but always passed it by a hundred bounds. And then they had to dash back to the stopping place.

In this fashion they reached Toola.

Platov did not get out of his coach, but sent one of his orderlies to fetch the gunsmith in whose hands he had left the steel flea. He was so impatient that he at once sent another orderly after the first, and yet a third one after him. And so he dispatched them one after another, till all his orderlies had been sent off. Then Platov was reduced to dispatching people out of the crowd that had gathered about his coach. In fact, he was almost ready to leap out of the coach himself, so great was his impatience.

When the orderlies arrived at Lefty's house, they banged on the door, but there was no answer. Then they tried the shutters. But the shutters were fastened tight. They pulled at the door. But it was bolted from inside with an oaken bolt and did not give even a fraction of an inch. There was nothing more to do but to fetch a log and place it under the eaves and lift off the roof. And without more ado this was what they did. But the air that escaped from the room where the three gunsmiths had been working, with door and windows shut tight, was so stifling that it knocked out the orderlies. As soon as they came to, they picked themselves up and shouted: "You scoundrels! What do you mean by knocking folks down?"

"One minute," called Lefty. "We're driving in the very last little nail. When that's done, we'll bring out our work."

"While you're doing that," groaned the orderlies, "our General will eat us alive!"

"He won't have time to swallow you," said Lefty. "As you were speaking we drove in the last little nail. Run and tell him that we are coming with the job."

The orderlies ran ahead, looking behind them as they went. Sure enough, the gunsmiths were following them, fastening the hooks of their kaftans as they came. Two of the gunsmiths were empty-handed. But the third, Lefty, was carrying, wrapped in green velvet, the Czar's traveling case, which held the golden snuffbox, which held the diamond walnut, which held the steel flea.

The orderlies dashed up to Platov's coach.

"Here they are, your Honor!" they panted.

"Is it finished?" Platov asked the gunsmiths.

"All finished, your Honor," they answered in chorus.

"Then let's have a look at it."

So Lefty handed the traveling case to Platov. Meanwhile the coachman took his seat on the box, and the two Cossacks sat on either side of him, with their nagaikas lifted, ready for use.

Platov snatched the traveling case, tore off its green velvet cover, took out the golden snuffbox and out of the snuffbox the diamond walnut. He opened the diamond walnut and saw the steel flea lying there just as it had always lain. There was nothing else there.

"What's this!" shouted Platov. "Where is your work? What have you done to deserve the trust of our Emperor?"

"Our work's right there, your Honor," said the gunsmiths.

"But what is it?" Platov demanded.

"It's there, right before your eyes," said the gunsmiths. "You've only to take a look."

Platov shrugged his shoulders angrily. Then he shouted: "Where is the key to the flea?"

"It's right there, your Honor," said the gunsmiths as before. "Where the flea is, there the key is, all in one nut."

Platov wanted to get hold of the key, but his fingers were too stubby. He tried and he tried, but he couldn't grasp either the flea or the key that wound it up. Suddenly he got even angrier and began to curse in true Cossack fashion.

"You scoundrels!" he bellowed. "You've done nothing at all! Maybe you've even ruined the Czar's flea. I'll have you beheaded!"

"You are the Czar's envoy, your Honor," said Lefty, in a huff. "Have us beheaded, if you please. But don't insult us."

Platov snorted.

"You think we would try to cheat the Czar!" Lefty went on indignantly. "We are Toola men! As to the work we've done," he said with hurt pride, "we're mum."

"Mum!" roared Platov. "I'll make you talk!"

Lefty only replied: "Be so good as to take the flea to the Czar. Let him look at her. He'll see whether he has cause to be ashamed of us."

And no matter how much Platov fumed and threatened and wheedled, there was nothing to be got out of the men.

"You scoundrels!" Platov shouted finally. "I'm not going to let you get away with this. I'll take one of you with me to the capital. I'll get to the bottom of your rascality!"

With that he grabbed Lefty so roughly that all the hooks and eyes flew off his kaftan. Then he threw Lefty into the coach at his feet.

"Sit there like a poodle," growled Platov, "till we get to St. Petersburg. You'll answer for the lot."

"But where's his passport? He can't travel without a passport!" cried Lefty's comrades.

"There's his passport," said Platov, showing his fist, all slashed from the wars. "And now let's be off," he said to the coachman. "Day after tomorrow we must be in the capital."

So saying he gave the Cossack to the right of the coachman a shove with his boot and the Cossack to the left of the coachman a shove with his other boot. The Cossacks at once began belaboring the coachman, the coachman began belaboring the horses, and they bounded away.

THEY went even faster than before, so fast that Platov's brains were joggled. And the joggling turned up new ideas in Platov's head. "Suppose," he thought, "these bunglers have ruined the steel flea! When I take it to the Czar, and he deigns to look at it, his sharp eyes will at once detect the damage. And then not only will the gunsmiths of Toola be disgraced, and the Russian people along with them, but I, General Platov, will have to hang my head in shame and go from the august presence with my tail between my legs, as it were."

This thought was so horrible to Platov that he got redder than ever and gave the Cossacks on the box an extra kick apiece. With this, the flogging was renewed and the horses speeded up and Platov was bounced about and his brains bounced inside his head and he got another idea.

"Suppose," he thought, "instead of going directly to the capital, I take the steel flea back to England and show it to the English craftsmen! If anything is wrong, they will know it, and perhaps I can even get them to patch it up somehow. In any case, I will have this squint-eyed son of a sea-cook basted within an inch of his life!"

The more he thought about it, the better Platov liked this project. So at once he ordered the coachman not to halt at St. Petersburg, but to drive straight on until they reached England.

"And mind you," Platov roared, "go fast when you approach the Channel. Then the horses will cross it in one jump, or, at the most, in two."

"Just as you say, your Honor," murmured the coachman. And away they raced, stopping but for food and drink, and that only when Platov grew hungry. He was too impatient to have a good appetite. In this way they soon arrived in England.

Platov went at once to the works where the steel flea had been forged.

The English workmen welcomed him heartily. And they inquired most particularly as to what Emperor Nicholas had said when he saw the delicate example of English know-how bequeathed to him by his late brother.

"Oh," answered Platov carelessly, "the Emperor Nicholas graciously condescended to admire your work. Indeed," said Platov, "he was pleased to observe that it was very good. For English work." Platov paused a moment. The Englishmen did not seem sufficiently gratified. Besides, it was a ticklish business to get them to look at the flea without telling them the whole story about the gunsmiths of Toola. And this he did not want to do. He did not like to admit to the Englishmen that Russian workmen might have ruined the steel flea. He cleared his throat and cast a warning glance at Lefty.

"Yes," he went on. "His Majesty even had it shown to our gunsmiths at home."

"Indeed!" exclaimed the Englishmen.

"Yes," said Platov. "Yes. But," he cleared his throat again, and again glanced threateningly at Lefty, "but I am not sure if our Russian climate agreed with your steel flea. We have snowstorms in Russia, you know, regular blizzards that would freeze the whiskers off you English. And in summer it is so delightfully hot that those unaccustomed to our Russian sun might just melt away. It may have affected the works of your steel flea. Anyway, I have brought her here for you to have a look at her. Please examine her and see if she is all in good order."

"Now," thought Platov to himself, "if Lefty here has improved on the steel flea, we shall have put one over on the

English. And if he has spoiled the thing, why, I shall find out, but the English will think it's only our climate."

Thereupon he opened the traveling case, took out the golden snuffbox, removed the diamond walnut, opened it, and disclosed the steel flea. When the Englishmen saw her again, they could not contain their delight.

"Well, that really is something!" they exclaimed. "We did a good job when we made that!"

They lifted her carefully out of the diamond walnut, and then they looked for the key. But Platov had left the microscope at home, so they had to fetch another one in order to find the key. Meanwhile they examined the steel flea. Platov watched them with his eagle eyes to see whether they noticed anything new about the flea. But he could tell nothing from their expression. At last a microscope was brought, but before they looked for the key, they trained it on the steel flea. And then indeed, as one Englishman after another looked at it, his eyes got rounder and his mouth opened wider.

"Well," growled Platov impatiently. "What are you gaping at?"

"Extraordinary!" muttered the Englishmen. "Fabulous! Impossible!"

"Has the flea been tampered with?" Platov thundered.

"Your Honor," said the Englishmen, rubbing their jaws in wonder, "this is beyond belief!"

Platov did not understand what they were talking about.

"Has our Russian climate affected the steel flea?" he asked grumpily.

"Your Honor," said the Englishmen, "it doesn't look like the work of the climate. It looks like . . ." But without finishing the sentence, they all sighed in amazement.

"Wind her up," Platov said, "and see what happens."

So the Englishmen took the key and wound up the steel

flea. She was the same, yet not the same. True, she made a step to the right and then she made a step to the left. But she did it all slowly.

Platov was enraged. First he gave Lefty a thrashing. Then without waiting to see why the steel flea behaved in this fashion, he snatched it up, and the key with it, stuck them into the diamond walnut, thrust the walnut into the snuffbox and the snuffbox into the traveling case, and ignoring Lefty in his haste, bade the Englishmen farewell. Then he went to his lodgings, took out his pipe, lay down on the couch, and wrapped himself in clouds of smoke, as though to hide from the disgrace that had befallen the Russian people.

Platov had no sooner departed than the English workmen crowded around Lefty.

"The old man doesn't even know why the flea moves slowly. He must be blind! But not us, matey. We know good work when we see it. And you're prime!"

Lefty let them make a fuss over him and take him about and show him the weapons they had made, all very interesting to a Toola gunsmith. They were anxious to keep such a fine craftsman. They plied him with food and drink. They even offered to find a wife for him. But Lefty thanked them politely and said he preferred to remain a bachelor. As a matter of fact, he was homesick.

MEANWHILE, Platov had been lying on the couch in his lodgings, smoking his pipe, and only now and then fortifying himself with some vodka and a crisp cucumber. But this could not go on forever. One fine day he got up, threw his pipe into the corner, shook himself, and said: "I must report to the Czar."

It was a terrible thought. This brave veteran of a score of battles trembled at it. But what must be, must be. So he sent his orderlies to scour the city for Lefty, tie him up, and fetch him to Platov's lodgings.

The orderlies did as they were bidden. Lefty did not like being tied up, and he did not look forward to Platov's company, but if all this was necessary in order to get back home, he could put up with it.

Having made up his mind to return, Platov lost no time. And as soon as they reached St. Petersburg, he put on all his medals and decorations, tucked the traveling case under his arm, and went to the palace, taking Lefty along with him.

When they entered the palace, Lefty remained below in the foyer, while Platov went on upstairs. As soon as he got to the top of the stairs, he quietly placed the traveling case behind the stove in the anteroom. "If the Czar happens to remember the steel flea," he said to himself, "of course, the matter will have to be taken up. But if he forgets about it, then I need say nothing. The Czar's valet can put the traveling case away in some cupboard or other. And as for Lefty, I'll throw him into a dungeon and he can stay there until he's wanted."

Then Platov went to present himself to the Czar. This took immense courage. Platov had never flinched before the fiercest enemy. But when he thought of showing himself to the Emperor and the possibility of being asked about the steel flea, his knees shook and his throat went dry. Nevertheless, like the brave old soldier that he was, he marched on until he reached the Emperor's study.

As soon as Platov had greeted the Czar, he began to report

on how things were on the quiet Don. He thought that the Czar would be distracted by his account. But the Czar never forgot anything. When Platov had finished his report on the quiet Don, Emperor Nicholas asked: "Well, what have our Toola masters done about the English flea?"

"The flea, your Majesty," answered Platov, turning slightly pale, "is just as it was. I have brought it back with me. The Toola men have not been able to produce anything more remarkable."

"You are a brave old man," said Emperor Nicholas, "but what you are telling us cannot be so."

Platov assured the Czar that it was so, adding that, nevertheless, the Toola gunsmiths had bidden him show the Emperor the flea.

At that the Czar clapped Platov on the shoulder and said cheerfully: "Good! Bring it here. We know that our Russian people will not fail us. They must have produced something."

So the traveling case was taken from its hiding place behind the stove and brought to the Emperor. The green velvet cover was removed, the golden snuffbox taken out of the traveling case, the diamond walnut inside it was opened, and there lay the flea, just as the Emperor remembered her. He looked at her, and murmured in a tone of disappointment: "So that's how it is."

But his faith in his Russian masters remained firm.

He summoned his favorite daughter, the Princess Alexandra Nikolayevna.

"You have delicate fingers, my dear," he said to her. "Take the tiny key and quickly wind up the spring in the middle of this flea."

The Princess managed to get hold of the tiny key with her delicate fingers, and she inserted it in the flea's middle and turned it round and round. At once the flea's whiskers began to twitch, but the legs remained motionless. Princess Alexandra Nikolayevna continued winding, and at last the flea moved her limbs slightly. But her movements were clumsy and she was quite unable to perform the figures of the quadrille.

Platov turned green.

"Ah, those dogs!" he shouted. "What have they done! It's lucky I brought one of them with me. He'll answer for it before your Majesty!"

With these words he dashed out, ran downstairs, clutched Lefty by the hair, and began to pull him about so that the hair came out in handfuls. When Platov paused for breath, Lefty smoothed himself out, and said: "When I was an apprentice, my master pulled out the hair at my temples. But I don't know why you have to pull out the rest now."

"It's because I put my trust in you," answered Platov angrily, "and I recommended you. And you ruined a fine piece of work! And now the Czar knows it too!"

"We're grateful to you that you went surety for us,"

said Lefty. "But we didn't ruin anything. You've got to look at it with the most powerful microscope."

"That beating I gave you isn't all you'll get for this!" Platov threatened Lefty. Nevertheless he ran back to report to the Czar about the microscope. But first he told the orderlies to tie up Lefty more tightly.

Then Platov started upstairs again, panting, and murmuring a prayer under his breath.

The courtiers who flanked the staircase turned a cold shoulder on him, whispering to one another: "Ah, Platov is in disgrace! Platov is going to be chased out of the palace!" They liked the idea, because they were jealous of the brave old soldier.

Platov went on into the Emperor's study and reported to him what Lefty had said. At once the Emperor exclaimed joyfully: "We knew that our Russian people would not fail us!"

And he ordered that a microscope be brought in.

Immediately a microscope was served on a cushion. The Czar took the steel flea and put her under the lens, first with her back up, then with her belly up, then on one side, then on the other side. In a word, she was turned over and over and looked at from every angle, but there was nothing to be seen. Even then the Czar did not lose faith. He only said: "Bring me this gunsmith who is down below."

"But your Majesty," Platov objected, "the man isn't decently dressed. He is just as I took him from the forge. And besides, at present there are other reasons why he isn't fit to be seen."

"Never mind," said the Emperor. "Bring him as he is."

So Platov went down to Lefty and told him: "You're to go before the Czar, you unthinkable thought of an unspeakable word. Go before the Czar, and answer for what you've done!"

"All right," said Lefty. "I'll go. I'll answer for it."

And so he went. His clothes were ragged, and one trouser leg was tucked inside his boot and the other hung outside. His kaftan was shabby and minus hooks and eyes, and his collar was torn. But Lefty was not embarrassed. "And if I have no passport," he said to himself, "I can't help it. I can explain." But he was relieved when Platov had the orderly untie him so that he could be admitted to the presence of the Czar.

Lefty went in and made a low bow. And at once the Czar asked him: "Well, brother, what's wrong? We've looked at the steel flea this way and that way, and we even put her under the microscope, and yet we saw nothing remarkable about her."

"Did you get a proper squint at her, your Majesty?" asked Lefty.

The courtiers made faces at Lefty to signify that he wasn't speaking as he should before the Czar. But the Czar only said: "Leave him alone. Let him express himself as he knows how." Then he graciously explained to Lefty: "We placed the steel flea like this." And he put her under the microscope. "Look for yourself. You won't see anything different about her."

"You can't see it proper like this, your Majesty," replied Lefty. "Because our work is much too fine."

"How shall we be able to see it then?" asked Emperor Nicholas.

"Well," said Lefty, "you've got to put just one of her legs under the microscope at a time and look carefully at each foot on which she steps."

"You don't say so!" exclaimed the Czar. "That's a remarkably small thing to look at!"

"Can't be helped," said Lefty. "That's the only way your Majesty can see what we've done."

So they placed the steel flea exactly as Lefty directed.

No sooner did the Emperor put his eye to the lens than he fairly beamed. He took Lefty just as he was, unkempt, unwashed, ragged and dusty, into his arms, embraced him, and kissed him on both cheeks. Then he turned to the courtiers and said: "You see! We knew better than anyone that our Russian workmen would not fail us. Pray look into the microscope! These rascals have shod the English flea! They've given her horseshoes!"

Everybody came up to look. Indeed, each one of the steel flea's hooves was shod with a real little horseshoe! But when

they all exclaimed over it, Lefty said that this was not the most marvelous thing that the Toola masters had done.

"If you had a stronger microscope," he said, "one that makes things about five million times bigger, then you'd see that on each horseshoe is engraved the name of the master who forged it!"

"And is your name here too?" asked the Czar.

"No, not mine," said Lefty. "My name's missing."

"How is that?" asked Emperor Nicholas.

"Because," Lefty answered with a grin, "I worked at something a good bit smaller than the flea's horseshoes, your Majesty."

"And whatever could that be?" the Czar asked in wonder.

Lefty leaned toward the Czar, cupped his hands around his mouth, and whispered something into the imperial ear.

"No!" cried the Emperor in astonishment. He stared at Lefty for a full minute without speaking. "And what sort of microscope did you use?" he asked.

"We're poor folk, your Majesty," Lefty answered. "We're too poor to own any microscopes. But what we have got, your Majesty, is a trained eye."

"Train my eye!" commanded the Czar.

"Just take a squint, Sire," said Lefty. "Like this."

The Czar squinted at one of the flea's horseshoes. Then he shook his head.

"I can't see it," he said sadly.

"Take another squint, Sire," Lefty begged him. "Like this."

The Czar looked again.

"Y-ye-es . . . yes. YES!" he cried out.

And he was so overjoyed that he at once commanded that Lefty be treated to the best that the palace had to offer, and be provided with a uniform.

The courtiers, seeing that Lefty had won the Czar's favor with his work, embraced him and made much of him. But they could not imagine what it was that he had done.

They crowded around respectfully, wondering what it could be. Platov twirled his mustachios and stood on tiptoe, trying to see over the heads of the rest.

"Get along with you!" cried the Czar, waving them away, "and do as we bade you."

So they took Lefty's dusty, sooty, ragged clothes away, gave him a steam bath, and dressed him in the elegant uniform of a Court Singer, the only one that fitted him. Platov himself went up to Lefty, saying gruffly: "Forgive me, brother, for pulling you about like that before."

"The Lord will forgive you," said Lefty. "It's not the first time that happened to me."

"But," Platov whispered, "what was it really that you made?"

"Why don't you ask the Czar?" replied Lefty with a wink.

"I will," vowed Platov.

Then they took Lefty back to the Emperor.

The Emperor's eyebrows were still raised in astonishment, and he was sighing with rapture over Lefty's wonderful work.

Finally Platov made bold to speak.

"Sire," he said, clearing his throat, "will it please you to tell us just what work the honorable Lefty did on the steel flea?"

The Czar smiled.

"Believe it or not," he answered, "Lefty forged the nails with which the horseshoes are fastened on. You can see for yourself."

At that there was a loud huzzah, and everybody embraced Lefty all over again and began loading him with presents. Platov himself gave Lefty a hundred rubles. And he received many other magnificent gifts besides.

But that was not all.

One fine day the Czar summoned Lefty and said to him: "Brother, we have done everything we could think of to honor you as you deserve for your wonderful work, and to make you happy. But perhaps we have not guessed right as to how to please you best. Now we want you to tell us the wish of your heart. Don't answer at once. Think it over carefully, and when you are sure that you know what it is, come and tell us."

Lefty made a low bow and answered that he did not need to think it over at all.

"You are quite sure?" asked Emperor Nicholas.

"Sure," said Lefty, "your Majesty," he added politely.

"Well, then, what is the wish of your heart?"

"To go back home to Toola," said Lefty promptly.

And so the Czar gave him leave to go home, and he went.

He was received with rejoicing by all the folk of Toola, especially by his two fellow workmen, with whom he shared his good fortune. Everyone was full of talk about Lefty and proud and glad to have known him so long. Only one person took it all very quietly. That was Lefty's old mother. She just looked at her son, folded her hands over her stomach, smiled to herself, and said: "I told you so!"